Freddie Fernortner

FEARLESS FIRST GRADER®

An AudioCraft Publishing, Inc. book

Book storage and warehouses provided by Chillermania!©
Indian River, Michigan

Freddie Fernortner, Fearless First Grader
Book 11: Tadpole Trouble
ISBN 13-digit: 978-1-893699-29-8

Cover and illustrations by Cartoon Studios, Battle Creek, MI
Text and illustrations copyright © 2010, AudioCraft Publishing, Inc.

AMERICAN CHILLERS® , MICHIGAN CHILLERS® and FREDDIE FERNORTNER, FEARLESS FIRST GRADER® are registered trademarks of AudioCraft Publishing, Inc.

Dickinson Press Inc., Grand Rapids MI, USA • Job 3899100 July 2011

TADPOLE
TROUBLE

VISIT CHILLERMANIA!

WORLD HEADQUARTERS FOR BOOKS BY JOHNATHAN RAND!

CHILLERMANIA!

**I-75 Exit 313
then south
1 mile!**

Visit the HOME for books by Johnathan Rand! Featuring books, hats, shirts, bookmarks and other cool stuff not available anywhere else in the world! Plus, watch the American Chillers website for news of special events and signings at *CHILLERMANIA!* with author Johnathan Rand! Located in northern lower Michigan, on I-75! Take exit 313 . . . then south 1 mile! For more info, call (231) 238-0338. And be afraid! Be veeeery afraaaaaaiiiid . . . .

1

Freddie Fernortner, fearless first grader, was excited. So was Chipper, one of his best friends.

But Darla—another one of Freddie's best friends—wasn't all that thrilled.

You see, the three friends had decided to look for frogs in a nearby pond. Freddie and Chipper wanted to catch one, but Darla didn't. She didn't like frogs.

"I think all frogs are icky," she told

Freddie and Chipper.

"Frogs aren't icky," Chipper said. "They're cool."

"Yeah," Freddie said. "It would be fun to catch one."

"I'm not touching any frog," Darla said, shaking her head. "I'll help you look, but I'm not going to get close."

Together, they walked the short distance to the pond. Freddie's cat, Mr. Chewy, followed, happily chewing his gum and blowing bubbles.

The pond wasn't very big. It was surrounded by bushes and cattails. There was a long dock that went out over the water. The sun was shining, and the sky was blue. A few birds chirped, and a light wind caused the cattails on the other side of the pond to sway gently.

The three first graders stopped at the edge of the pond.

Freddie pointed. "Let's look over there," he said, "on the other side of the pond."

"I can't wait to catch a frog!" said Chipper. "I caught one last summer at the park."

"I hope he doesn't bite you," Darla said. "Frogs don't bite!" Chipper and Freddie both said at the same time.

"My brother says frogs have big teeth," Darla said.

"Your brother is just fooling you," said Chipper. "He just wants—"

Suddenly, Freddie pointed into the water and shouted. "Look!" he cried. "Look at that!"

Chipper and Darla looked at where Freddie was pointing, and the three first graders were amazed at what they were seeing.

2

Sitting on a log was a large turtle! The sun glistened on his shiny, dark shell, and he watched the three first graders watching him.

"He's cool," Freddie whispered.

"He's awesome," Chipper whispered.

"What if he attacks us?" Darla asked softly.

Freddie and Chipper both laughed. "Turtles don't attack people!" Freddie said.

The laughter scared the turtle, and he suddenly slipped off the log and vanished into the water.

"Let's see if we can find a frog," Freddie said.

The three first graders took off their shoes, removed their socks, and rolled up their pant legs. They waded slowly into the pond, their eyes gazing into the water.

"Do you see anything, Freddie?" Chipper asked.

Freddie shook his head. "Not yet," he said. "Do you see anything, Darla?"

"Nope," Darla said. "I just see a bunch of weeds and rocks."

They searched and searched. Even Mr. Chewy helped. He sat in the grass at the edge of the pond, chewing gum, blowing bubbles, and looking for a frog.

"I want to catch a big bullfrog," Freddie said.

"We have to find one first," said Chipper. "But I don't see any."

"If I get attacked by a frog, you guys are going to be in big trouble," Darla said.

"Darla," Freddie said, "I promise you: frogs don't bite. They won't hurt you."

Nearby, the turtle's head popped up in the pond. He watched the three first graders as they waded in the water, looking for frogs. Then, he dipped his head beneath the surface and vanished again.

But while Freddie, Chipper, and Darla were searching for frogs, something was searching for them.

Something that wanted blood.

Suddenly and without warning, the creature attacked . . . and bit Darla's leg!

3

Darla screamed. Freddie and Chipper, still wading in the water, spun around.

"What's the matter?" Freddie shouted.

Darla looked at her leg, where a large mosquito was biting her. She slapped at it and missed, and the insect buzzed off and vanished.

"It was only a mosquito!" Chipper said, shaking his head. "You screamed so loud that

I thought you were being bitten by a shark."

"He was trying to suck all of the blood out of me!" Darla protested.

The three first graders continued searching, but they didn't find any frogs. Mr. Chewy hadn't spotted any frogs, either.

"Maybe they all went to the store," Chipper said. "You know, to pick up some frog food."

Freddie laughed. "I don't think frogs go to stores," he said. "I think they stay around ponds where they can eat bugs for free."

"I'm getting bored," Darla said, placing her hands on her hips. "If we don't find any frogs soon, I'm going home."

"We have to be patient," Chipper said. "Frogs are good at hiding. They blend in with the green weeds."

"That's right," Freddie said. "There

might be a frog watching us at this very minute, but he's hiding, and we can't see him."

"I don't want frogs spying on me," Darla said.

Freddie was looking down at his feet, into the water, when he saw something move. He was curious, and he bent over for a closer look.

Suddenly, he gasped.

"Guys!" he whispered excitedly. *"Come here! Come here and look at this!"*

4

Darla and Chipper waded over to Freddie. Water sloshed at their ankles. Mr. Chewy stood, but he stayed on the shore and chewed his gum. He didn't like water.

At Freddie's feet, small, dark creatures, no bigger than a penny, swam about. They had round heads and a thin tail, but no arms or legs. They looked like tiny minnows with big heads.

The three first graders watched them curiously.

"Are they fish?" Darla asked.

Freddie shook his head. "I don't think so," he said.

Suddenly, Chipper gasped and spoke. "I know what those are!" he said excitedly. "They're tadpoles!"

"Tadpoles?" Darla asked. "What's a tadpole?"

"Tadpoles turn into frogs!" answered Chipper.

"Those little things turn into frogs?" Darla asked. "How?"

"First," Chipper said, "they grow hind legs. Then, they grow front legs, and their tails shorten. My dad told me."

Darla put her hand on her hips. "Are you making this up?" she asked. She thought

Chipper was trying to fool her.

"No, he's not," Freddie answered as he shook his head. "Chipper's right. They're tadpoles. In time, they'll grow into frogs." Suddenly, Freddie's eyes widened, and his smile stretched across his face.

"I have an idea!" he blurted. "Let's catch some and take them to my house! We can keep them in our fish tank and watch them turn into frogs!"

"That's a great idea, Freddie!" Chipper said.

"What if something goes wrong?" Darla asked.

"What could go wrong?" Freddie asked. "All we have to do is feed them and watch them grow. Nothing can go wrong."

At least, that's what Freddie thought. Because lots could go wrong. In fact, the three first graders were soon going to find themselves in big, big trouble!

5

The three first graders raced back to Freddie's house and returned to the pond with some small butterfly nets and pails. The tadpoles didn't swim very fast and were easy to catch. Soon, Freddie, Chipper, and Darla had caught a bunch of tadpoles.

"What are we going to do with them now?" Darla asked.

"We have a big, empty fish tank,"

Freddie said. "Mom and Dad used to raise tropical fish, but they don't anymore. It will be perfect for our tadpoles!"

They carefully carried the pails of tadpoles to Freddie's house, put them in the fish tank, and watched the tiny creatures swim around and play like little underwater monkeys.

"What do they eat?" Darla asked as they gazed at the tadpoles through the glass.
"I think they eat leaves and weeds," Freddie said. "Let's find out."

They went outside, gathered some green leaves, and returned. Freddie placed a handful of leaves in the tank, where they floated at the surface.

"Look!" Darla said. "They're eating the leaves!"

Darla was right! The tadpoles swam up

to the leaves and munched on them with their tiny mouths.

"They're pretty hungry," Chipper said. "I wonder how long it will take before they turn into frogs?"

"I think it takes a few weeks," Freddie said. "Maybe longer."

Days passed. Each morning, Freddie would slip out of bed, walk to the fish tank, and peer inside to see if the tadpoles had grown. Each morning, he would call Chipper and Darla on the phone and tell them the same thing.

"Nope," he would say. "Nothing yet. They still look the same."

And then, one day, something very, very magical happened . . .

6

One morning, Freddie approached the fish tank. Mr. Chewy followed, but he wasn't chewing gum yet. It was still too early in the morning. Freddie and his cat looked into the aquarium.

Suddenly, Freddie's eyes grew very, very wide.

The tadpoles had grown tiny hind legs overnight!

"Wow!" Freddie said as he watched the happy creatures swimming about. "How about that, Mr. Chewy? They're growing! They're turning into frogs!"

Freddie raced to the phone to call Chipper and Darla, and it wasn't long before they, too, were standing in the Fernortner's living room, staring in wonder at the small, dark green tadpoles and their newly-grown legs.

"Their legs aren't fully grown," Freddie explained. "But they will be, soon!"

"How cool!" Darla said.
"I didn't think they were ever going to grow," said Chipper.

"It just takes time, that's all," Freddie said. "They still have a lot of growing to do. But we can watch them as they get bigger and bigger!"

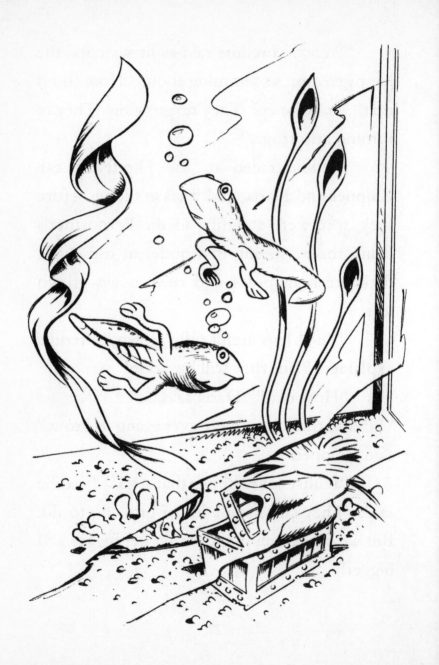

Each day, Darla and Chipper would walk to Freddie's house, where the three of them would gaze at the tadpoles in the tank. Each day, the tadpoles grew more and more. Soon, front legs began to grow, and their tails began to shorten. The creatures started to grow bigger, too, and continued gobbling up the green leaves that Freddie placed in the fish tank each day.

Finally, after a few more weeks, the tadpoles weren't tadpoles anymore. They had changed completely and turned into frogs.

But that was when the trouble was about to begin. You see, raising tadpoles is quite easy. But raising frogs? Well, that's much, much different. And the three first graders were quickly going to find out that big trouble was about to start hopping!

7

Freddie, Chipper, and Darla realized one thing: the aquarium wasn't big enough for all of the frogs. They were no longer tiny little creatures. Each had grown to the size of a golf ball, and there were just too many in the aquarium. They made the decision to take twelve frogs to the pond to let them go. They would keep the remaining twelve frogs in the aquarium and watch them grow.

One day, while Freddie, Chipper, Darla, and Mr. Chewy were watching the frogs swimming and floating in the aquarium, Freddie had an idea.

"Hey," he said, "why don't we take our frogs to school for show and tell?"

"That's a great idea!" Chipper exclaimed. "Yeah!" said Darla. "We could tell everyone about how tadpoles turn into frogs!"

"We could even make a chart with drawings," Freddie said.

They went to work. Using a big piece of cardboard, they created a picture board to show the different stages and life cycle of the frog. The more they worked on their project, the more excited they became.

"Our friends in class will learn a lot about frogs," Chipper said.

"I used to think frogs were icky," Darla said. "Now, I think they're really cool! I've learned a lot about tadpoles and frogs."

"Me, too," Freddie said.

But there was one thing that the three first graders hadn't thought about. As the frogs grew, they became stronger. Their legs became more powerful. Soon, they were able to leap very high . . . which meant that they would be able to leap out of the fish tank.

And one day, when no one was watching, that's exactly what happened.

One frog sprang up, leaping over the side of the glass fish tank and landing inside Mrs. Fernortner's purse. Another frog jumped out, landed on the table, made several leaps, and landed in Mr. Fernortner's briefcase.

Mrs. Fernortner didn't know there was a frog in her purse.

Mr. Fernortner didn't know there was a frog in his briefcase, and that morning, he closed his briefcase, carried it to his car, and drove to work. Although it was Saturday, and he normally didn't work on weekends, he had a very important meeting to attend.

The neighbor lady, Mrs. Huffsnuffle, arrived to watch Freddie for a couple of hours while his mother was away at her luncheon. Things were about to go crazy.

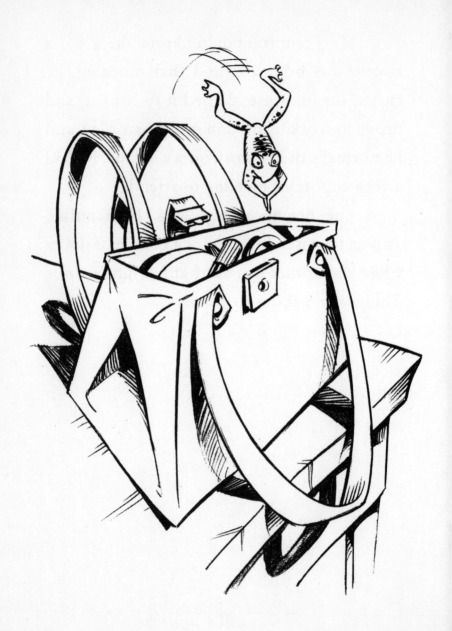

8

"My son, Freddie," Mrs. Fernortner was saying, "has had so much fun." She was sitting in a restaurant at a table with her friends, Mrs. Peterson and Mrs. Barr. The small group was sipping iced tea and eating lunch. "He and a couple of his friends raised tadpoles into frogs," Mrs. Fernortner continued. "They learned a lot, and they've even put together a show and tell presentation for school. I'm very proud of them."

"Why, how wonderful!" Mrs. Peterson said.

"Yes," said Mrs. Barr. "I've always thought your son was a very smart boy."

Mrs. Fernortner was about to take a bite of her sandwich . . . when the unthinkable happened. The frog that had been hiding in her purse suddenly leapt out. It landed on the table and sat, staring with glossy dark eyes at the three ladies.

Mrs. Fernortner shrieked and covered her face with her hands.

Mrs. Peterson was so frightened that she nearly fell out of her chair.

Mrs. Barr gasped.

"Oh, my!" Mrs. Fernortner said. "One of Freddie's frogs must have gotten loose! It's been hiding in my purse!"

The frog jumped again. He made one bounce on the table before making another jump, and this time he landed on Mrs. Barr's shoulder! Mrs. Barr, surprised and horrified, fainted right then and there.

Mrs. Peterson began fanning poor Mrs. Barr with her handkerchief, trying to revive her. Meanwhile, the frog sat on her shoulder, staring blankly around the restaurant. The small creature had no idea what all the fuss was about.

Mrs. Fernortner didn't know what to do. She'd never had a frog leap from her purse before.

Mrs. Peterson continued fanning Mrs. Barr. A waiter came over to help, but the frog suddenly leapt from Mrs. Barr's shoulder and landed on the waiter's tray!

But if things at the restaurant had gone

crazy, it was nothing compared to what was about to happen at Mr. Fernorter's office.

9

Mr. Fernortner was seated around a big table with three other men, talking about business. It was an important meeting.

"As I was saying," Mr. Fernortner continued, "I have my report here in my briefcase. I've been working hard on it for a couple of weeks."

"I'm excited about this project," Mr. Fernortner's boss said. "I can't wait to see what your report says."

The briefcase was sitting on the table. Mr. Fernortner reached for it and flipped up the two levers to open it.

"I made copies for all of you," Mr. Fernortner said. "That way, we can all read it together."

He lifted the lid of his briefcase.

At that very moment, the frog that had been hiding inside made a giant leap. Papers went flying as the green creature made one bounce . . . and landed on the head of Mr. Fernortner's boss! The frog sat perched in his hair, looking around the room.

Mr. Fernortner and the two other men looked on, staring at the frog sitting on their boss's head.

"My goodness!" Mr. Fernortner said. "I have no idea how that could have happened!"

Mr. Fernortner's boss was angry. "Do you always carry small green frogs in your briefcase?" he demanded.

"I'm so sorry, sir," Mr. Fernortner said. "My son, Freddie, has been raising frogs. One must've escaped. Hold on, and I'll catch him." Mr. Fernortner reached out and plucked the frog from his boss's head. Then, he scooped up his paperwork and placed the frog and the papers in his briefcase.

"I'm so very sorry about this," said Mr. Fernortner. "I'll take the frog home right away and come back to the office in a few minutes."

At the Fernortner house, Mrs. Huffsnuffle was in the living room, reading a book. Freddie, Chipper, Darla, and Mr. Chewy were sitting on the porch, working on their show and tell frog project. As fate would have it, Mr. Fernortner arrived home in his car, followed by Mrs. Fernortner in her car.

The cars pulled into the driveway.

They stopped.

Mr. and Mrs. Fernortner got out.

And they weren't very happy.

10

Mr. and Mrs. Fernortner got out of their cars and approached the porch. Mr. Fernortner was carrying a briefcase, and Mrs. Fernortner was carrying a small brown bag. Freddie knew something was very wrong, because his father wasn't supposed to be home from work until later in the day, and his mother was home early from her luncheon.

"Freddie," his father said sternly, "do

you know where all of your frogs are?"

"Yeah," Freddie replied. "They're in the fish tank in the living room."

"Well, then," Mr. Fernortner said, "how do you explain this?"

He knelt down, placed the briefcase on the porch, and opened it. Inside, a green frog sat, staring back at them with beady, black eyes.

Darla's eyes grew wide. "Mr. Fernortner!" she gasped. "You stole one of our frogs!"

Mr. Fernortner shook his head. "No, I didn't," he said. "It must've escaped from the fish tank and hopped into my briefcase."

"Not only that," Mrs. Fernortner said, "but another one got into my purse. It jumped out while we were having lunch and landed on Mrs. Barr's shoulder. Poor Mrs. Barr fainted!"

"That's horrible!" Chipper said. "Our poor frog was probably scared to death!"

Mrs. Fernortner frowned. "The waiter had to catch the frog and put him in this bag," she said. She handed the paper bag to Freddie. Carefully, Freddie peered inside the bag and saw the green frog looking up at him.

"If you're going to keep frogs in the house," Mr. Fernortner said, "you're going to have to make sure they don't escape."

"We will, Dad," Freddie said. "I'm really sorry."

"Yeah," Darla said. "It won't happen again."

You would think that would have been the worst of their problems. But for Freddie Fernortner, fearless first grader, and for his friends Chipper, Darla, and Mr. Chewy, the trouble was only beginning.

11

Days passed, and the frogs continued to grow bigger and bigger. Finally, the big day arrived: the day when Freddie, Chipper, and Darla would take their frogs to school for show and tell.

"This will be so much fun!" Darla said as she, Chipper, and Freddie walked to school. Chipper was carrying the big piece of cardboard that showed the life cycle of the frog. Darla was carrying a book about frogs that she'd borrowed from the library, and Freddie was carrying a brown bag. Inside the bag was a glass jar containing a frog. A lid was screwed on the top of the jar, and holes had been poked into it so the frog could breathe.

When they arrived at school, a crowd gathered around the three first graders. Everyone wanted to see the frog, but Freddie kept the creature hidden in the bag. He wanted it to be a big surprise.

"I wish I was in your class, Freddie," someone said. "I'd like to learn all about how tadpoles become frogs."

"Me, too," someone else said.

The first bell rang, telling the students that they needed to be on their way to their classrooms. Soon, school would begin.

"I can't wait!" Darla said. "This will be

the coolest show and tell ever!"

"No one else has ever brought a real, live frog into school before," Chipper said. "I bet everyone is going to love it!"

"I've been waiting for this day for weeks," Freddie said. "This is one of the most exciting days of my life!"

But there was one thing that the three first graders didn't know. They didn't know that that morning, while Freddie was carefully placing one of the frogs in the jar, another one had escaped from the aquarium. It had leapt onto the counter, where it sat for a moment before making one giant jump, landing inside Freddie's lunchbox . . . where it hid beneath a peanut butter and jelly sandwich wrapped in wax paper.

Freddie, of course, was completely unaware of the frog in his lunchbox . . . and later that day, in the school cafeteria, he and his classmates were going to get a big surprise!

12

When Freddie, Chipper, and Darla arrived at their classroom, Freddie gave the bag containing the jar and the frog to his teacher, who placed it in a cupboard behind her desk for safekeeping. Chipper leaned the big sheet of cardboard against the wall at the front of the classroom with the life cycle facing the wall so no one could take a sneak peek. Darla placed the frog book on her desk.

They were ready.

At twelve o'clock, the lunch bell rang. As the students in Freddie's class got up to go to the cafeteria, their teacher stood.

"Freddie, Chipper, and Darla," she said. "Are you ready for show and tell after lunch?"

"We can't wait!" said Freddie, and the three first graders snapped up their lunchboxes and joined their classmates as they filed down the hall to the cafeteria.

"I can't wait until lunch is over!" one of their classmates said. "I want to see that frog!"

"Our whole class is excited about our project," said Darla.

"That's because it's so cool," Chipper said. "Everybody wishes that they had raised tadpoles like we did."

While they walked, the three first graders talked about their show and tell project.

"Chipper," Freddie said, "you and Darla hold up the cardboard to show our drawings. I'll hold up the jar with our frog, and we will all take turns reading from the cardboard. Then, I'll walk around the classroom to let everyone get a good look at our frog."

"Everyone will be amazed that our frog began as a little tiny tadpole," Darla said.

They rounded a corner and turned into the cafeteria. Many of their classmates were already seated at tables, smiling and laughing, chatting with one another. Other students were in line at the lunch counter.

Freddie, Darla, and Chipper found their usual place at their usual table.

"What kind of sandwich do you have today, Freddie?" Darla asked.

"Peanut butter and jelly," Freddie replied as he placed his lunchbox on the table.

"My mom made me a salamander sandwich," Chipper said with a smile. "Salamanders are delicious."

Darla winced. "Eww," she said. "That's so gross."

Freddie turned his lunchbox toward him. He flipped open the latch, then opened the lid. He spoke. "I can't wait until—"

Suddenly, something burst from the lunchbox. Something green. Something that moved very fast, surprising the three first graders.

Freddie, already realizing what had happened, tried to capture the frog before it got away . . . but it was too late. Things in the cafeteria were about to get crazy.

13

The frog landed on the table, and Freddie sprang to capture it. Scared by the sudden movement, the frog jumped again, landing in a tray of food! The girl seated behind the tray screamed.

"It's a monster!" she shrieked as she ran off. "It's an ugly, green monster from outer space!"

This, of course, caused all of the other

children to panic. None of them wanted to be attacked by an ugly, green monster from outer space. They leapt from their seats, many of them spilling food and milk onto the table, seats, and floor. Some of them screamed.

"It's not an ugly green monster from outer space!" Freddie said as he jumped to his feet. "It's only a frog! He won't hurt anyone!"

"Watch out! That thing has teeth!" someone yelled.

"He bit me twice!" someone else hollered.

"Frogs don't bite!" Chipper said as he, too, got up from his seat. "Don't panic! We'll catch him!"

By now, everyone in the cafeteria had fled the tables. They had heard about the ugly, green monster from outer space. They knew that it had sharp teeth and that it had already bitten someone. Of course, none of this had actually happened, but when people panic, their imaginations go wild.

Meanwhile, the frightened frog had made another leap and was now sitting on top of a sandwich on the table. He had no idea how much trouble he had created. He had no idea he was sitting on a ham sandwich, either.

" Chipper," Freddie said, "you get on that side of him, and I'll stay on this side. Let's move slow. One of us will be able to capture him. Darla, be ready with my lunchbox, so we can put him back inside where he can't escape."

Darla picked up Freddie's lunchbox and peered inside. She was worried that there might be another frog hiding in it. There wasn't. The only thing she saw was a wrapped sandwich, an apple, and a juice box.

"I'm ready," she said.

Freddie and Chipper were closing in on the frog, who was still seated atop the ham sandwich. Most of the students had run away, but a few curious ones had returned, wanting to get a closer look at the ugly, green monster with big teeth from outer space.

Then, Freddie sprang, covering the frog with both of his hands before it could leap away.

"I've got him!" he said. Quickly, he ran to Darla who was holding out the open lunchbox. He carefully dropped the frog inside and closed the cover.

"Whew!" Freddie said as he took the lunchbox from Darla. "I thought we were going to be in a lot of trouble!"

But Freddie spoke too soon. Suddenly, a big, booming voice echoed through the cafeteria.

"What's going on in here?!?!"

Every single student turned to see the school principal, Mr. Hugabee, as he entered the cafeteria.

"Uh oh," Freddie whispered. *"Maybe we're in trouble, after all . . . ."*

14

"Mr. Hugabee!" Freddie said quickly. "I can explain everything!"

But a girl at the far end of the cafeteria spoke up. "It was an ugly, green monster from outer space!" she said. "He attacked me! He tried to bite me!"

Chipper nodded and spoke. "That's right, Mr. Hugabee," he said. "It was an ugly, green monster from outer space. It's a good thing you came in when you did, because you scared him away."

Mr. Hugabee looked confused. "What is all of this talk about ugly, green monsters from outer space?"

"Oh, yes," Darla said. "He was horrible. But he's gone now, thanks to you."

Mr. Hugabee looked around the cafeteria. "Okay, everyone," he said loudly. "Take your seats and finish your lunches."

"That's right," Freddie said in a loud voice, glancing around the crowd of students. "The ugly, green monster from outer space is gone. There's no reason to be afraid."

Freddie, Chipper, and Darla returned to their seats. Soon, all of their classmates had cleaned up the messes and returned to their tables. Some of them looked around warily, wondering if they would see the green creature that had caused such a fuss. Most of them didn't know that it had been just a harmless frog.

"Now what?" Chipper asked. "You can't eat your lunch, because you'll let the frog out." "If I'm really careful," Freddie said, "maybe I can reach in, grab my sandwich, and close the lunchbox before he jumps out."

"I can't watch!" Darla said, and she covered her face with her hands.

Freddie placed his hands on the lunchbox. He flipped the latch and opened the lid a tiny bit. Then, very carefully, he reached his fingers inside and pulled out a sandwich, quickly closing the lid before the frog could escape.

"Great job!" Chipper said. "At least you won't starve."

"Let's finish our lunches," Freddie said

as he unwrapped his sandwich. "Then, let's go back to our classroom and get ready for show and tell before anyone else gets back."

They finished eating, cleaned up after themselves, and left the cafeteria. When they arrived at their classroom, it was empty.

"Mrs. Pugdoodle must still be eating her lunch," Chipper said.

"That's okay," Freddie said. "You and Darla get the cardboard display. I'll get the frog from the cupboard."

While Chipper and Darla went to the front of the class to pick up the cardboard, Freddie opened the cupboard. He pulled out the bag containing the jar with the frog.

But there was only one problem . . . and it was a big one.

The jar wasn't there!

"Oh, no!" He cried. "Our classroom

isn't the only thing that's empty. The bag is empty, too! Someone has stolen our jar and our frog!"

15

The three first graders panicked.

"Where did he go?" Chipper asked.

"I don't know!" Freddie cried. "But our frog and the jar are gone!"

"There's a frog thief in the building!" Darla said.

"This is horrible," Freddie said. "Our show and tell project is ruined. We don't have a frog to show!"

"Yes, we do!" Chipper said. He pointed at Freddie's lunchbox. "We've got a frog, right in there! In your lunchbox!"

"But what if he gets loose again?" Darla asked. "Then, we'll—"

Suddenly, Mrs. Pugdoodle walked into the room. She was carrying the jar containing the frog. When she saw the three first graders, she smiled.

"Oh! Hi, kids," she said. "I took your frog to the lounge to show the other teachers. I told them how you had raised him from a tadpole and that he was your show and tell project this afternoon."

"Whew," Freddie said with a sigh of relief. "Mrs. Pugdoodle, we thought someone stole our frog."

Mrs. Pugdoodle handed the jar to Freddie. "I'm sorry I worried you," his teacher said. "Are you ready to show your classmates?"

"Oh, yes!" Freddie said, and he placed the jar back into the paper bag just as other students began to arrive in the classroom. They took their seats, and within a few minutes, all was ready.

"Class," Mrs. Pugdoodle began, "I know we're all excited to see Freddie, Chipper, and Darla present their show and tell project. Most of you know what it's about, so I will let our three students take it from here."

The three first graders stood in front of Mrs. Pugdoodle's desk. Each one of them took turns reading about the life cycle of the frog, how it began as an egg in the pond, hatched into a tadpole, grew legs, and then turned into a frog. But the students couldn't see the frog in the jar, because it was still in the bag.

Finally, they finished reading from the big piece of cardboard. The special moment had arrived.

"All right," Freddie said proudly. "Who wants to see our frog?"

Hands went up throughout the classroom. Everyone wanted to see the frog. They couldn't wait.

Freddie turned and looked into the bag. A look of shock and horror fell over his face.

"Oh, no!" he said. "Our frog! He's gone!"

16

There were several gasps around the classroom. Chipper and Darla rushed to Freddie's side, peering into the bag.

Suddenly, Freddie smiled.

"Just kidding," he said, and he pulled the jar from the bag and held it out for his classmates so they could see the frog that had once been a tiny little tadpole in the aquarium.

Then, Freddie walked around the room so everyone could get a closer look. His classmates gazed at the frog in amazement and wonder. When he was finished, and everyone had been able to take a look at the frog, he returned to the front of the classroom.

"And that," he said as he took a bow, "is all about the life cycle of a frog."

Chipper and Darla bowed, too, and everyone in the class began to clap. Even Mrs. Pugdoodle was clapping.

"Excellent job!" the teacher said.

Freddie, Chipper, and Darla were very proud. They had worked hard on their show and tell project. Not only that, they'd had a lot of fun.

But while walking home after school, Chipper and Darla noticed that Freddie was very quiet. In fact, he looked a little sad.

"What's wrong, Freddie?" Darla asked.

But Freddie didn't say anything. He just continued walking.

"Freddie?" Chipper asked. "Is something the matter?"

Freddie stopped walking and looked sadly at his two friends.

"Yes," he said. He hung his head.

"What is it?" Darla asked. She and Chipper stopped walking.

"It's something we have to do," Freddie replied as he raised his head. "I don't want to, but we have to."

"What is it, Freddie?" Chipper asked. "What do we have to do?"

"Yeah," Darla said. "What is it, Freddie?"

Slowly, Freddie told them what needed to be done. Darla hung her head in sorrow.

Chipper was very sad, too.

But they knew that Freddie was right. What they were going to have to do now was going to be very difficult . . . and the three first graders were very, very sad.

17

What Freddie, Chipper, and Darla had to do was this:

They had to let the frogs go free.

Sure, they'd had a lot of fun raising them from tadpoles, caring for them every day. It was exciting to watch them grow legs and turn into frogs. They learned a lot, and it was an experience they would never forget.

But they also knew that the frogs belonged in the pond. That was their home. The frogs were wild, and while it was fun to take care of them for a short period of time, the place they really belonged was on their own, living in the pond.

So, later that evening, the three first graders gathered at Freddie's house. They put the frogs in a bucket and placed a block of wood on top so they couldn't jump out. Then, they carried the bucket across the street. Mr. Chewy followed, chewing his gum and blowing bubbles.

"You know," Freddie said as they stopped near the edge of the pond. "I was sad before, but now that I've thought about it, I'm really happy. I'm happy we got to see the tadpoles turn into frogs, and I'm happy that we were able to take them to school for show and tell. And I know that the frogs will be happy to be living in the pond. So, that makes me happy."

Chipper and Darla thought about this.

"You're right, Freddie," Darla said. "That makes me feel better, too."

"Me, too," Chipper said. "I was really sad, but I know that we're doing a good thing by letting the frogs go home. Besides, we can do it again next year, if we want. We can catch tadpoles and watch them turn into frogs again."

They emptied the bucket, and the frogs spilled out into the water. They seemed very happy to be in the pond, on their own.

When the three first graders were finished, they stood by the edge of the pond, watching the last few frogs kick their legs and swim away.

"Goodbye, guys," Freddie said with a wave of his hand. "Thanks for all the fun."

Freddie, Chipper, and Darla didn't want to admit it, but each of them cried just a tiny bit.

And that was okay.

"That was so much fun," Chipper said as they began to walk back to Freddie's house. "I don't think we'll ever have so much fun ever again."

"Oh, yes we will," Freddie said. "I know something that might even be more fun than raising tadpoles."

"You do?" Darla asked.

Freddie nodded and smiled. "You bet," he said.

"What could be more fun than raising tadpoles?" Chipper asked.

"Halloween," Freddie said smartly.

Darla frowned. "But Freddie, it's not even October. Halloween is a long ways away."

"But we've got to start planning now," Freddie said. "In fact, I've been thinking about the perfect costume."

"What are you going to be?" Chipper asked. "A vampire?"

Freddie shook his head. "No," he said.

"A zombie?" asked Darla.

Once again, Freddie shook his head. "Nope," he replied.

"What, then?" Chipper asked.

Freddie's eyes grew wide and bright. "I'm going to be a famous monster from the movies," he said. "I'm going to be Frankenfreddie!"

Darla scratched her head. "Don't you mean Frankenstein?" she asked.

Freddie shook his head. "Nope," he said. "I'm going to be Frankenfreddie, and I'm going to have the scariest monster costume ever."

And as it would turn out, Freddie would be right. His costume would be the scariest monster costume ever.

But what would happen to him—and Darla, Chipper, and Mr. Chewy—would be one of the most horrifying experiences of their lives.

NEXT:

FREDDIE FERNORTNER,

FEARLESS FIRST GRADER

BOOK TWELVE:

FRANKENFREDDIE

CONTINUE ON TO READ

THE FIRST TWO CHAPTERS

FOR FREE!

1

Halloween costumes can be funny. They can be silly and strange. Other Halloween costumes can be weird. Still, many costumes can be very, very cool.

But this isn't a story about one of those costumes. This is a story about Freddie Fernortner, fearless first grader, and a very terrifying Halloween costume. There is no doubt this story will scare many readers, so if you are easily frightened, you probably shouldn't read it. And even if you are very brave, don't ever read this story at night, as it might cause some very terrifying nightmares.

But if you are brave and aren't easily frightened, continue reading. Brave readers will find this to be a story with many thrills, scary surprises, and much excitement.

One day, Freddie and his friends, Chipper, Darla and Mr. Chewy were walking to a nearby park. Mr. Chewy, Freddie's cat, followed closely behind the three first graders, chewing his gum and blowing bubbles. Most cats don't like gum, but not Mr. Chewy. In fact, that's how he got his name.

"It's a beautiful day," Darla said as she gazed up into the blue sky. The sun was shining, and there wasn't a cloud in sight.

"It will be a great day to play in the park," Chipper said. "Maybe we will even meet some more of our friends."

"I hope so," said Freddie. "If we meet up with a few more of our friends, we might be able to play a game of basketball."

The three first graders and Mr. Chewy continued walking along the sidewalk. Suddenly, Freddie noticed something up ahead.

"Hey guys," he said, pointing. "Take a look at that."

At the end of the block, a new sign had been placed in front of a building . . . a building that had been empty for a long, long time.

"It looks like a new store is coming to that old building," Chipper said.

"What does the sign say?" Darla asked.

"I can't read it," said Freddie. "It's too far away."

They continued to walk closer and closer to the building.

Closer and closer to the sign.

Closer and closer to something they never saw hiding in the bushes, waiting for them . . .

2

The three first graders kept walking toward the new sign, trying to read it. Mr. Chewy scampered behind them, chewing his gum.

They stopped near a row of thick, dark green bushes that grew along the sidewalk. They had no idea hidden eyes were spying from inside the bushes.

Freddie stared at the sign in the distance, and spoke.

"I think it reads something about a

costume shop," he said.

"A costume shop?" Darla asked. "Like, Halloween costumes?"

"Probably all kinds of costumes," Chipper said.

All the while, the unseen eyes in the bushes watched and waited.

"A costume shop would be cool!" Freddie said excitedly. They might even have a Frankenstein costume! I can be 'Frankenfreddie' for Halloween!"

"What should I be?" Darla wondered aloud. "A fairy princess?"

"If you want," Chipper said. "You could be a fairy princess, and I could be a pirate! Or a zombie!"

"Maybe I could be a zombie princess!" Darla said. "That would be funny and scary!"

"I'll bet they have all kinds of different costumes," Freddie said. "You can be anything you want for Halloween."

"But Freddie," Darla said, "It's not Halloween, yet."

"That's why we should start looking for costumes right now," Freddie replied. "We need to find the perfect costumes before all of the good ones are taken."

All the while, as the three children chattered about Halloween, spooky nights, and scary costumes, they had no idea something was hiding in the bushes, waiting for just the right moment to leap out.

"Come on, guys," Freddie said. "Let's go see what kind of costumes they have!"

The three first graders and Mr. Chewy began walking again, and it was at that very moment the creature in the bushes made its move. It sprang from its hiding place so quickly that Freddie, Chipper, and Darla didn't even have time to scream for help.

ABOUT THE AUTHOR

Johnathan Rand is the author of more than 65 books, with well over 4 million copies in print. Series include **AMERICAN CHILLERS, MICHIGAN CHILLERS, FREDDIE FERNORTNER, FEARLESS FIRST GRADER,** and **THE ADVENTURE CLUB.** He's also co-authored a novel for teens (with Christopher Knight) entitled **PANDEMIA.** When not traveling, Rand lives in northern Michigan with his wife and three dogs. He is also the only author in the world to have a store that sells only his works: **CHILLERMANIA!** is located in Indian River, Michigan. Johnathan Rand is not always at the store, but he has been known to drop by frequently. Find out more at:

www.americanchillers.com

ATTENTION YOUNG AUTHORS!
DON'T MISS

JOHNATHAN RAND'S

AUTHOR QUEST®

THE DEFINITIVE WRITER'S CAMP
FOR SERIOUS YOUNG WRITERS©

If you want to sharpen your writing skills, become a better writer, and have a blast, Johnathan Rand's Author Quest is for you!

Designed exclusively for young writers, Author Quest is 4 days/3 nights of writing courses, instruction, and classes at Camp Ocqueoc, nestled in the secluded wilds of northern lower Michigan. Oh, there are lots of other fun indoor and outdoor activities, too . . . but the main focus of Author Quest is about becoming an even better writer! Instructors include published authors and (of course!) Johnathan Rand. No matter what kind of writing you enjoy: fiction, non-fiction, fantasy, thriller/horror, humor, mystery, history . . . this camp is designed for writers who have this in common: they LOVE to write, and they want to improve their skills!

For complete details and an application, visit:

www.americanchillers.com

WATCH FOR MORE FREDDIE FERNORTNER, FEARLESS FIRST GRADER BOOKS, COMING SOON!